SOCCER HERO

THE #1
SPORTS SERIES
FOR KIDS
®

SOCCER HERO

LITTLE, BROWN AND COMPANY
New York Boston

Little, Brown and Company
Hachette Book Group
1290 Avenue of the Americas, New York, NY 10104
Visit us at LBYR.com
mattchristopher.com

Originally published in trade paperback by Little, Brown and Company
in September 2007
New Edition: March 2021

Little, Brown and Company is a division of Hachette Book Group, Inc.
The Little, Brown name and logo are trademarks of Hachette Book Group, Inc.

The publisher is not responsible for websites (or their content)
that are not owned by the publisher.

Matt Christopher® is a registered trademark of Matt Christopher Royalties, Inc.

Text written by Stephanie True Peters

Library of Congress Control Number: 2007925431

ISBNs: 978-0-316-54213-5 (pbk.), 978-0-316-09433-7 (ebook)

Printed in the United States of America

LSC-C

Printing 1, 2021

1

Rob Lasher wiped the sweat from his brow and looked longingly at the jug of ice water on the bench beside the field. The sandy-haired twelve-year-old had been running drills with his soccer team, the Pirates, for more than an hour under the blazing September sun. The team's first game was in two weeks and Rob knew Coach Brennan wanted to be sure they were ready. Still, he couldn't remember ever being so hot and thirsty.

Just when Rob was sure he couldn't take it any longer, his coach let out a piercing whistle.

"Okay, men, five-minute break," Coach Brennan called. He joined the boys jogging off the field.

Rob filled his paper cup as full as he could, then stepped aside and began to sip the cool, refreshing liquid. Benji Lombardo was next to grab a cupful of water. But instead of drinking it, he dumped it on his head.

"You know, Benji," Rob said admonishingly, "you should get that *into* you, not *onto* you. I read that dehydration can cause dizziness. You don't want to collapse on the field, do you?"

Benji laughed. "I'll take my chances," he said.

Still laughing, he turned for a refill. Then suddenly, he staggered, dropped his cup, and grabbed the bench with one hand.

"I knew it!" Rob cried. "Benji, are you okay? Put your head between your knees so you don't black out!"

Benji opened one eye and grinned up at Rob. "Gotcha!"

Rob took a step back and grimaced. "Ha, ha, very funny. You know, Benji —"

"You know what I know, Rob?" Benji interrupted. "I know that if you say 'you know, Benji' one more time today, I'm going to hydrate your body with that entire jug of water!"

By now the whole team was laughing. Even Coach Brennan, a no-nonsense man with powerful arms, a trim waist, and strong legs, smiled.

"Hey, coach, want some water?" one of the players called. "You look like you've been running a marathon!"

Coach Brennan drew his hand across his forehead and stared at his sweaty palm in surprise. "I must be moving around out there more than I thought," he commented. "And you must be right about dehydration and dizziness, Rob. I'm feeling a little light-headed!"

He started to reach for a cup but stopped abruptly and grabbed his left arm at the bicep.

"Oof!" He straightened and rotated his shoulder. "Guess I didn't stretch out enough today. I think I just pulled a muscle!"

Most of the boys laughed at the thought of such a simple movement as reaching for a cup causing pain. Rob did, too, until he noticed that the coach was still wincing and rubbing his shoulder.

"You know, coach, it could be a pinched nerve in your neck or your back," Rob said. "I read somewhere that pain can be felt far from where the actual damage is."

"Mmmm." The coach sounded distracted. "Okay, boys, break's over. Back to the field for one more drill before we call it quits for today."

The team gave a collective groan.

"C'mon, I'll play, too," Coach Brennan added. "Maybe moving around will unkink my pinched nerve, or pulled muscle, or whatever this ache is!"

That stopped the grumbling. Many of the boys had been on Coach Brennan's soccer team for at least two years. They knew having the coach take part in drills made it more fun.

"Bryan, Ming, and Scott, you three will be defense," the coach said. "The rest of you, form two lines on either side of the center circle."

The defense took up fullback positions in front of the goal while the others lined up as instructed. Meanwhile, Coach Brennan arranged orange cones in two lines leading up to the penalty box.

"The offense is going to work on dribbling, dodging, and shooting," he said. "You'll take off two at a time, slalom through the cones, work past the defense, and then blast a kick into the net. The defense will work on double-teaming and on straight-on attacks. It'll be up to them to decide which of the two players coming toward them to double up against."

The coach jogged to the front of one of the lines and glanced at the boy at the front of the other. "Dmitri and I will go first, show you how it's done. After we shoot, the next two in line start the drill. Everyone ready? Then let's go!"

Dmitri, a tall thirteen-year-old with thick black hair, took off like an arrow released from a bow, toeing the ball expertly in and around the cones and having no trouble matching the coach's speed and finesse.

"Go, Dmitri!" shouted a young boy named Kirk. Kirk was new to the team. From the day he started practicing with the Pirates, he'd followed Dmitri around like a faithful dog. It was obvious he thought Dmitri was the greatest thing since sliced bread.

Not that Dmitri didn't deserve some admiration. He was the best player they had, a shoo-in for the position of starting center forward. For that reason alone, he'd probably be elected this year's team captain, too.

The coach made it through his cones a split second before Dmitri. Bryan and Ming raced forward to double-team him. While Coach Brennan dodged this way and that to avoid their attack, Dmitri beat Scott in a one-on-one match and booted the ball into the net.

"Whoo-hoo! Did you see that? That was some precision kicking, D-man!" Kirk held up his hand to high-five Dmitri. Dmitri gave him a light slap and then dropped the ball at his feet so he could take his turn.

It was Rob's turn, too. He wasn't as quick

or as nimble as Dmitri or the coach, but Kirk, who was slaloming through the other set of cones, was even slower. Ming and Scott chose to double-team Rob, leaving Bryan to cover Kirk alone.

But Rob had anticipated their move. He sidestepped Ming cleanly. In the next second, he had booted the ball past Scott, picked it up again behind him, and laced it into the goal.

"Yes!"

Rob pumped his fist and grinned. Behind him, Benji shouted. Rob turned, expecting to see his friend giving him the thumbs-up.

Instead, he saw Benji pointing a horrified finger to someone on the field.

Rob spun around just as Coach Brennan clutched his chest and crumpled slowly to the ground.

2

Oh my gosh!" Rob said as he and the others ran to the coach's side.

"Is he — is he *dead?*" Kirk whispered.

For a split second, Rob thought the answer to Kirk's question was yes. But then he added up everything the coach had been experiencing in the past ten minutes: the sweats, the dizziness, the sudden pain in his left arm and shoulder.

"He's having a heart attack!" Rob cried. "Call 9-1-1!"

As Scott ran for his cell phone, Rob knelt down beside the coach and tried to roll him onto his back. But the coach was too heavy for him to move alone. "Someone give me a hand here! I've got to start CPR."

"Wha — what's CRP?" Kirk's voice quavered; the young boy was on the brink of tears.

"CPR, not CRP! It stands for cardiopulmonary — oh, never mind! Just *help* me, someone!" Together, Rob, Kirk, and Ming rolled the coach over. The man's face was gray.

Benji ran up then. "Scott called 9-1-1. An ambulance is on the way!"

Rob took a few deep breaths then and recalled the three basic steps — the ABCs, as they were known — of cardiopulmonary resuscitation.

"*A is for airway;* make sure it's open."

He put his hand under Coach Brennan's neck and carefully tilted the head back so that the coach's chin was pointing up. He listened for the sound of air going in and out of the coach's mouth. He didn't hear anything.

"*B is for breathing.* Get oxygen into him!"

He pinched Coach Brennan's nose shut with one hand. He inhaled, covered the coach's mouth with his own, and exhaled. Then he did it again.

"His chest went up! He's breathing!" Kirk cried.

Rob didn't bother to point out that he, Rob, had breathed for the coach. He was too busy feeling for a pulse in the coach's neck. He didn't find one.

"*C is for circulation.* We need to get the heart pumping!"

There was a specific spot on the coach's chest where he was supposed to apply steady beats of pressure with his overlapped hands. As he searched for it, he heard the wail of a siren in the distance.

"That's the ambulance," Benji said.

"I have to begin CPR anyway," Rob said. "Every minute counts." He found the spot, laid one hand over the other, and laced his fingers together. Then, with his elbows locked and his full weight behind him, he began to push rhythmically on Coach Brennan's sternum. He counted out loud as he did.

"*One*-and-*two*-and-*three*-and-*four*-and-*five*-and-*six*-and-*seven* . . ."

He continued the rhythm until he'd reached fifteen. Then he delivered two more breaths into the coach's mouth before returning to his chest again.

He was midway through the second cycle of beats when he heard a deep voice say, "We'll take it from here, son."

Rob had been concentrating so hard he hadn't heard the ambulance arrive or the emergency medical technicians approach. Now two strong hands covered Rob's smaller ones. Together, the paramedic and Rob finished the fifteen-pulse count. Then Rob stepped back to let the man do his job. Meanwhile, the other EMT was readying some frightening-looking equipment.

It was like watching a scene from an emergency room drama show. But this wasn't any TV program — this was real life. The *coach's* life.

Rob sat down hard as that realization struck him.

The paramedics worked on Coach Brennan for a few minutes. Then, to everyone's relief, Coach Brennan gave a low moan that signaled his return to consciousness. The EMTs advised him to lie still while they lifted him onto a stretcher. Then, with Rob and the others following, they carefully carried the coach to the ambulance and loaded him in. Just before the back doors closed, one of the paramedics yelled out the name of the hospital where they were taking the coach. Then the ambulance sped off with the siren screaming and the lights flashing.

As Rob watched the vehicle disappear around a bend, he felt his last bit of energy drain out of him. He lay down on the nearest bench, scrubbed his hands over his face, and closed his eyes.

A shadow fell over him. He opened his eyes again. To his surprise, he found himself surrounded by his teammates, all of whom were staring at him with open mouths. He sat up.

"What?" he said.

"What do you mean 'what?'!" Kirk cried. "You just saved the coach's life!"

"He's right," Benji seconded. "Rob, you're a hero!"

3

For a moment Rob was too dumbfounded to say anything. Then he began to protest. "I'm not a hero! I —"

But he didn't get a chance to finish what he wanted to say because, to his extreme mortification, Kirk started clapping. One by one, the others joined in until they were all applauding him like crazy.

Rob wished the earth would open up and swallow him whole. When the clapping continued, he jumped up, pushed through the circle of players, and ran off the field.

He didn't stop running until he was safe

inside his house. He leaned back against the front door, trying to catch his breath. Then he pushed off and started for his room.

"Whoa, Rob, take off those mud-packed cleats before you go another step!"

The voice came from the living room. Rob turned to see his mother frowning at him from the computer.

But for once, Rob didn't care if he made his mother upset. He just shook his head and ran upstairs to his room. He slammed his door, threw himself onto his bed, and covered his head with his pillow.

Some hero, he thought.

He lay still for some time. Then he heard the sound of a telephone ringing. A few minutes later, his mother knocked on his door.

"Rob? Can I come in, please?" Her voice was much softer than it had been earlier.

He pulled the pillow from his head and rolled over. "Sure."

His mother sat next to him. "Oh, honey. Benji's mom just told me what happened."

Rob's face twisted. "It was awful, Mom. One minute the coach was fine. Then it was like he was . . . was dead or something."

Mrs. Lasher stroked his hair. "But he's not, is he? And from what I heard, he has you to thank for that."

Rob gave a half shrug. "Probably he should thank you. You're the one who signed me up for that CPR class, remember?" He shook his head. "I just wish the guys hadn't started clapping and calling me a hero! It made me feel all weird, especially since Coach Brennan was being hauled away in an ambulance!"

Mrs. Lasher drew him close and hugged him. "I think they just couldn't believe what they'd seen you do. I'm a little stunned myself. And very proud, too, by the way. I know your father will feel the same way."

17

Mr. Lasher worked for a group that helped communities that had suffered through disasters. His job often took him away from home for weeks, sometimes months at a time. This time, he was near the Gulf of Mexico, overseeing reconstruction of communities that had been nearly wiped out by a huge hurricane. Even though Rob knew the work his father did was very important, he still missed him.

Rob and his mom sat in silence for a little while longer. Then Mrs. Lasher looked at her watch and sighed. "I have to get dinner started," she said. "Want to help me?"

Rob shrugged. "Yeah, I guess."

As he stood up to join her, the phone rang again. His mother hurried into the hallway to answer it. After speaking a few words, she held the receiver out to him.

"Rob, it's for you."

He took the phone and she continued down the stairs to the kitchen.

"Hello?" he said.

"Rob? This is Mrs. Brennan, Coach Brennan's wife."

Rob clutched the phone tightly. "Is — is the coach okay?"

"He will be, Rob, but he's going to need surgery to correct a defect with his heart."

"That's terrible!"

"Yes." Rob heard her take a deep breath. "I wanted to thank you, Rob, for what you did for him today. I don't know how we can ever repay you. The paramedics said your quick action probably saved his life."

The weird feeling came over Rob again, leaving him tongue-tied. He finally mumbled that he was glad he'd helped.

"Anyway," Mrs. Brennan said now, "I thought you should be the first to know. My

19

husband is going to have to resign from his post as your soccer coach."

"Oh," Rob said. "Who's going to take his place?"

Mrs. Brennan didn't say anything for a minute. Then, "Rob, I'm not sure anyone *is* going to take his place. It's so close to the start of the season, anyone who would be interested or qualified is probably already busy with another team. Chances are, the league will decide to reassign you and your teammates to other squads. If they can, that is."

Soccer was very popular in Rob's state. His town alone had five middle school teams made up of boys ranging from ages eleven to fourteen. These teams played against one another and against teams from neighboring towns.

Rob had played soccer on Coach Brennan's team the year before and had been psyched to find he was on his team again.

Although they'd only had a week's worth of practices together so far this season, he believed that he, Benji, Dmitri, and the others had the chance to be something special on the field. The last thing he wanted was to have to start all over again with players and a coach he didn't know — assuming he'd even be able to, that is.

But compared to what the coach was going through, how could he complain?

"I'm sorry to deliver the bad news," the coach's wife was saying. "And I hate to ask, but do you think you could call the rest of the team and let them know the situation? I'd like to get back to the coach's bedside."

"Sure, you bet. Tell him I hope he feels better real soon."

Rob set the phone back into its cradle and stared at it for a long minute. Then he went downstairs for dinner.

✿   ✿   ✿

Rob put off calling his teammates until the next morning. He contacted Benji first.

"Hey!" Benji cried. "How's the hero?"

"Cut that out, will you, Benji?" Rob growled.

Benji started laughing but stopped abruptly when he heard what the coach's wife had told Rob the night before.

"Aw, man, I don't want to get split up," Benji moaned. "No one but you guys appreciates my fancy footwork!"

Rob had to smile at that. Benji's "fancy footwork" usually found him tangled up with the ball and landing flat on his face. "I don't want to go to a new team either. But what can we do? If that's what the soccer league says we have to do, I guess we have to do it."

Benji was silent for a moment. Then he said, "I wonder if they'd let us look for our own coach? Just because they don't have anyone doesn't mean we can't find someone, right?" Excitement grew in Benji's voice. "Listen, before we give up, let's get everyone together and see if we can come up with some ideas on how to find a new coach. I'll call the offense, you call the defense. Tell whoever you get ahold of to meet at the field in half an hour. Oh, and tell them to wear their soccer stuff so we can play a pickup game, at least."

"Okay, I'll try," Rob said. He pressed the END button on the phone and then hit TALK to dial the first player's number. "But I don't know if it'll work," he said to himself.

4

Half an hour later, Rob joined his team-mates on the field. Out of the fourteen members, only four players — Dmitri, Joey, Rudy, and Scott — were missing.

"All right," Benji said when they all had gathered under the shade of a big tree. "We need a plan."

"Yeah," Kirk said. "Rob, what do you think we should do?"

Rob blinked in surprise. "Why're you asking me? Benji's the one who called the meeting!"

"Actually, Rob," Benji said, "maybe it

24

makes sense for you to tell everyone what Mrs. Brennan said first."

Rob nodded and told them about his conversation with the coach's wife.

"I'll bet she thinks you're the greatest!" Kirk said enthusiastically.

"Gotta admit, Rob, what you did was kind of unbelievable," Ming seconded. "So come on, you got any ideas for finding us a new coach?"

"Well, um, let's see," Rob mumbled awkwardly. "We could try putting up signs in some stores to let people know we're looking for a new coach."

Even as he suggested it, he thought it was a lame idea. Yet to his astonishment, his teammates nodded and smiled.

"And how about an ad in the newspaper?" Rob continued, now warming up to his ideas.

Now Benji jumped up. "I know just who to call. My sister's boyfriend's mother works for the *Town Gazette*. I'll bet she could tell us what to do. Of course, ads cost money. Would you guys be willing to chip in some cash to keep the Pirates together?"

Everyone nodded in agreement.

"Then I'll call the soccer league and make sure what we want to do is okay with them," Benji said.

"So, now that that's decided" — Rob picked up his soccer ball, lobbed it into the air, and bounced it off his knee — "how about we get a game going?"

Cheers of enthusiasm greeted the suggestion. The boys quickly divided into two teams. They flipped a coin to see which side would be skins. Rob's team lost, so he, Arnold, Sam, Benji, and Bryan shucked their shirts and headed for the field.

"Hey, Rob, should we use goalkeepers or just go without?" Kirk called.

"I vote go without," Rob replied. "That sound good?"

But Kirk didn't offer an opinion. Instead, he cried, "Rob says to play without goal-keepers!"

Rob opened his mouth to add that it was fine with him if others wanted to use goalies. But everyone seemed to agree with the decision, so he closed his mouth again and jogged toward his usual left midfield position.

He didn't reach it, however, because Benji shoved him toward the center circle instead.

"Go ahead, start things off," Benji yelled as he moved to his own spot at right midfield.

Rob had never played center forward before, but he knew what he was supposed to do. He put the ball on the ground, signaled the start of the game, and booted a sideways kick to Sam on his right.

Sam was a chunky boy with short legs. He

wasn't a great athlete, but he always tried his hardest. Now he controlled the ball and dribbled forward a few steps before passing back to Rob.

Rob saw an opening on the field. He dribbled toward it, only to have the opening close up when Brendan leaped to that spot. That left Arnold free. So Rob booted the ball to his other forward and then darted ahead in case Arnold sent a return pass.

The pass back did come, but so hard and so fast that Rob wasn't prepared. The ball ricocheted off his shin and careened over the touchline.

"Our throw-in!" Ming called.

As Ming started toward the ball, a tall boy with dark hair scooped it up. "Heard you guys were pulling together a pickup game. So who's winning?"

It was Dmitri. Scott was with him, too.

"Excellent!" Leo exclaimed. "Now that you guys are here, we can play six-on-six!"

"And guess what?" Kirk chimed in. "Rob came up with these great ideas for finding us a new coach!" He quickly filled them in on what had been discussed — praising Rob way more than Rob thought he should have. "So, Rob," he finished, "which team should they go on?"

But Dmitri was already pulling off his shirt. "I'll be on skins. Scott, how about you do us all a favor and keep *your* shirt on?"

"Ha, ha," Scott said sarcastically. But he trotted to the opposite side of the field.

Ming held out his hand. "It's shirts' throw-in."

Dmitri tossed him the ball and moved toward the center forward position.

"Um, Dmitri?" Rob said. "That's where I was playing."

29

"You were?"

"Yeah, but you take it. I'll switch to midfielder."

Dmitri gave him a long look. "That's all right," he said at last. "I'll try my luck at midfield." He moved to Rob's usual place at the left side of the field.

Ming lifted the ball behind his head and, with a strong two-handed throw, hurled it to his teammate, Raul.

Raul was the second-fastest dribbler after Dmitri. He took off at a fast pace, but Dmitri was even faster. He drew alongside Raul, poked his foot at the ball, and stripped it away.

It all happened so fast, Raul didn't seem to realize he no longer had the ball. By the time he did, Dmitri had passed up to Arnold, who held the ball for just a moment before blasting it to where Rob was waiting.

Rob took it on the fly. He dodged past

Brendan and then, with the goal in sight, drew his foot back for the kick.

He knew the minute his foot struck the ball that the kick was way off. The ball cleared the top of the goal by more than five feet! He stopped short, put his hands on his knees, and blew out his breath in disgust.

"Nice try!" Benji called. "Six feet lower and it would have been in for sure!"

Everyone laughed as they got ready to put the ball back in play. Since Rob had sent the ball over the goal line, it was shirts' goal kick. Brendan placed the ball in the goal area. Ming lined up to his right within the penalty box, Kirk to his left. Leo and Scott hurried to the corners of the box while Raul danced back and forth along the top. Their object was to clear the ball as far from their own goal as possible.

Rob and his team, meanwhile, were looking to do just the opposite. They drew in tight, but when Dmitri stepped inside the box, Rob held up his hand to halt play.

"Dmitri?" he said hesitantly. "The offense has to be outside the box for a goal kick, remember?"

The look Dmitri gave Rob this time was level and cool. But he moved so he was no longer within the penalty area. "Is that better?" he asked, his voice mocking.

Rob caught the tone, reddened, and looked away.

Benji caught the exchange. "Okay, you two, knock it off," he said. "Go on, Brendan, play ball!"

So Brendan drew his foot back and booted a solid kick to Raul. Raul trapped it just inside the box. As he did, Leo and Scott took off down the sidelines. Raul waited half a beat and then blasted the ball to Scott. Scott controlled it and dribbled toward the middle of the field.

Dmitri rushed him. So did Sam.

"Sam, I've got it!" Dmitri cried.

But Sam couldn't put on the brakes in time. The two players collided just as they reached Scott.

"Ooof!" Dmitri sprawled face first, his bare chest sliding across the rough grass. The ball bounced across the field and out of play.

"Man, are you okay?" Scott asked as he hurried to his friend's side.

Dmitri sat up. He looked irritated, and he had a long scratch near one of his ribs.

"Take a breather, dude," Leo said.

But Dmitri shook his head. "So, how are we going to rule that?" he asked as he brushed bits of grass from his chest.

"Are you kidding?" Scott said. "Sam fouled you!"

"They're on the same side," Rob pointed out. "So it can't be a foul."

Scott crossed his arms. "Okay, then what do you do when your own teammate deliberately trips you? Because that's what Sam did!"

"I did not!" Sam sounded surprised and hurt by the accusation. "I was going for the ball!"

"That was Dmitri's move to make, not yours!" Scott said, his voice rising. "He even told you to back off!"

Now Kirk stepped forward and put his hands on his hips. "Since when is Dmitri in charge? I say we let Rob decide!"

Rob, horrified by what was happening, started to protest. "No, wait, I —"

Dmitri held up a hand to cut him off. "No, no, I think you should decide, Rob. You seem to be the one everyone's listening to today."

5

Until that moment, Rob had never really understood the phrase "tension so thick you could cut it with a knife." Now, with the eyes of his teammates boring into him, waiting for his reply, he got it one hundred percent.

"Uh, hold on, let's see," he mumbled. His mind whirled as he tried to come up with a solution. Then finally, after what seemed like minutes but was probably only a few seconds, he thought of something.

"Let's do a drop ball to restart play right here where the collision occurred. Dmitri and Scott should battle for it, since it happened on

Dmitri's side of the field. I think that would be the fairest thing to do, anyway," he finished.

No one said anything for a moment. Then Brendan shrugged. "Sounds good to me. I'll drop it if you guys want."

And just like that, the tension lifted. Brendan held the ball in the air between Dmitri and Scott while the rest of the players scattered to their positions.

"Okay, ready?" Brendan called. He pursed his lips, whistled sharply, and let the ball drop to the ground.

Dmitri and Scott stabbed at it with their feet. Scott got control, but he didn't dribble far, for Sam suddenly came to life and stripped the ball from him with one smooth move. Seconds later, Sam scored.

"Whoo-hoo!" Benji yelled. "Take that, shirts!" He started chanting a fight song and doing a little dance.

Normally, Benji's antics made them all

laugh. But this time, only some of the kids were grinning. Dmitri and Scott were not among them.

Benji faltered in midchant. When he caught Rob looking at him, he gave a small, embarrassed shrug. Then he returned to his position on the field.

Raul, meanwhile, took the ball to the center circle where he and Leo had a quick whispered conference. Play resumed when Raul jabbed the ball to Leo. Leo dribbled down the center of the field with Raul trailing behind him by several paces.

Dmitri started toward Leo but then stopped when Benji moved in as well. But Benji slowed down at the same time, as if to let Dmitri make the play.

That hesitation gave Leo and Raul the time they needed to work the play they'd been whispering about. First Leo dribbled a few more paces. Then he left the ball behind but continued on down the field as if he still had possession.

The drop fooled both Dmitri and Benji for a split second — plenty of time for the fleet-footed Raul to rush forward, take control of the ball Leo had left for him, and dribble past them to the goal.

Sam rushed forward to break up the drive, but it was Bryan who saved the day. He planted himself in front of the goal, and when Raul took a shot, Bryan deflected it — right off his head!

The hit was so hard that it knocked him off his feet. He lay on the ground, stunned, while the ball soared into the air. When it came down, Raul was one step closer to it than Rob. All Raul had to do was tap it into the net.

Raul didn't celebrate the score, however. He held his hand out to Bryan and helped him to his feet instead. "Sorry!" he said. "I was aiming for the corner, not for you!"

"Yeah?" Bryan rubbed his forehead where a red mark was forming. "You got lousy aim, man!"

The two players stared at each other for a moment. Rob held his breath. Was this the start of another argument?

Then Raul and Bryan started laughing. Relieved, Rob did, too, and by the time the rest of the team had joined them, the three were howling.

They played for another half hour with the two teams exchanging goals, praise, and insults. Then, when there was a lull in the action, Benji said, "I think I've had enough soccer for one day. Who's up for a swim in my pool?"

The invitation was greeted with whoops of enthusiasm that quickly died when Benji added, "Admission to the pool is a couple of bucks."

"You're going to charge us to swim in your pool?" Sam asked, amazed.

"It's for the ad in the newspaper, clown!" Benji said. "If you bring your money now, it'll save me from having to bug you for it later!"

With that, the boys left for their homes. Rob's and Benji's houses were in the same direction, so they took off together.

"Was it just me," Rob asked as they hurried along the sidewalk, "or was Dmitri kind of mad at me today?"

Benji was quiet for a moment. Then just as they reached his house, he said, "I think Dmitri is used to having other players look up to him. Take Kirk, for example. Usually, he's Dmitri's number one fan. But today . . ."

"Today what?" Rob pressed.

Benji climbed the steps to his front door. "Today, Kirk had a bad case of hero worship!" He gave his friend a lopsided grin. "Not that you don't deserve it. In fact, if I had my way, the whole world would know about what you did for the coach!"

6

The swim party at Benji's house was a huge success, and not just because Benji's pool was the best one around. Benji had made good on his promise to call the soccer league, and by the time everyone had arrived, he'd gotten permission to put an ad in the paper. He'd called some stores, too, and been told he could post signs in their windows. And when all the money the boys brought had been counted, they had just enough to run a quarter-page ad in the paper.

"Now all I have to do is call the newspaper

back and place the ad," Benji said. "But that can wait until later." He pointed to a table where some pieces of fluorescent green poster boards and black markers were lying. "Right now, I'm going to work on those signs. Who wants to help me?"

But the other boys were more interested in swimming, so Benji wound up making the signs by himself. "I can swim anytime," he reasoned when Rob tried to get him to join in the fun.

The gathering lasted until sunset. Rob was exhausted from swimming and soccer, so when Benji asked if he'd help him post the signs after dinner, Rob shook his head.

"Okay," Benji said, "I guess I'll put them up myself after I call the newspaper about the ad."

Rob grinned. "Where do you get your energy, man?"

But Benji just waved him away. "Well, it's not like I'm using it to save lives or anything!"

Rob rolled his eyes and left.

Later that night, Rob had just finished putting away the supper dishes when the doorbell rang. A woman he'd never seen before stood on the other side.

"Hello!" she trilled, holding out her hand for him to shake. "You simply must be Robert Lasher!"

The woman's fingernails were long and pointed, like claws. After he shook her hand, Rob surreptitiously wiped his palm on the seat of his pants.

"Um, do I know you?" he asked.

"Maybe, maybe not!" The woman winked. "Do you ever read the newspaper, young man?"

"Sometimes. Sports section, I guess. Oh,

wait! Are you selling subscriptions or something? Because if you are, you should really talk to my mom, not me."

The lady laughed as if he'd told the funniest joke she'd ever heard. But she became businesslike when Rob's mother joined them.

"Mrs. Lasher, hello. I'm Enid Carmichael; I'm sure you've heard of me?"

Mrs. Lasher frowned slightly. "Why, yes, I believe I have. Don't you write articles for the *Town Gazette,* Ms. Carmichael?"

Ms. Carmichael looked delighted. "I do! That's why I'm here!" She crouched down and took Rob's hand in hers again. "A little bird called me tonight and told me about the very brave thing you did. Why, you're a real hero, Mr. Robert Lasher! And now the newspaper has authorized me to write your story — with your parents' permission, of course," she added hurriedly with a quick glance at Rob's mother.

Rob frowned. Who would have told her about what he'd done? Then suddenly, he remembered something Benji had said earlier that day:

If I had my way, the whole world would know about what you did for the coach!

Rob's heart started racing. Had *Benji* sent the reporter his way?

"Ms. Carmichael," Mrs. Lasher was saying, "we appreciate that you think your readers would find what happened interesting. However —"

Ms. Carmichael dropped Rob's hand and stood up before Rob's mother could finish. "Before you turn me away, consider this: every parent who reads Rob's story will wonder if their own children would have been able to do what he did. Most, of course, will know they couldn't have."

She took a step closer to Mrs. Lasher. "Wouldn't it be wonderful if after people read my article, they enrolled their children, perhaps even *themselves*, in such life-saving classes?"

Then she turned to Rob. "Here's another thing to think about: your team needs a new coach, right?"

Rob nodded. He figured Benji had told her about that, too.

"Well," the reporter said, beaming, "what better way to get the word out than a newspaper?"

Rob wasn't crazy about spending any more time with Ms. Carmichael. She was a little scary. But if it would help the team . . .

He looked up and shrugged. "Yeah, okay, I'll do it."

The delighted smile returned to the reporter's face. She spread her arms wide and for one horrid moment Rob thought she was going to hug him. Instead, she brought her hands together in a single clap.

"Marvelous!" she cried.

The interview took less than an hour, but to Rob it seemed endless. Ms. Carmichael asked him question after question after question — about CPR, soccer, the coach, his teammates, *everything*. When she finally closed her notebook, Rob was exhausted. But then she took out a digital camera and asked him to pose for some photos. Only after she had a shot that satisfied her did Ms. Carmichael gather her things to leave.

"Cross your fingers that we make tomorrow's paper!" she called as she climbed into her car. "Good-bye!"

Mrs. Lasher closed the front door and sagged against it. "Phew! That was tough for me, and I wasn't even the one answering her questions!" She rumpled Rob's hair. "I do believe we've earned ourselves big bowls of ice cream. With sprinkles!"

Rob was just scraping the last bit of

melted ice cream from his bowl when the phone rang. It was Benji.

"Guess what!" he cried.

"Hmm, let me think," Rob answered sarcastically. "You talked to someone at the newspaper?"

"That's right." Benji sounded surprised. "I put the posters up in the stores, too. But how did you find out about the paper?"

"Ha, ha, very funny," Rob responded. "Listen, Benji, I appreciate what you're trying to do. But next time, leave me out of it, okay?"

Benji didn't say anything for a moment. Then, "Gee, Rob, I thought you were on board with it. Sorry if we got our signals crossed."

"Yeah, well, next time, double-check with me first, okay?"

"Ooo-kaay," Benji said slowly. "Well, I guess I'll see you tomorrow at school. Um, good night."

"Yeah, good night."

7

Rob had been in bed reading for fifteen minutes when the phone rang again. His mother answered it and then opened his door, phone in hand.

"It's for you," she said.

"Is it Dad?"

Mrs. Lasher shook her head. "No, but trust me, you want to take this call."

Rob took the phone. "Hello?"

"Howdy, son," a man with a gravelly voice said. "I'm Stan Benoit. I'm the Pirates' new coach."

Rob sat up straight, stunned. "No way! Really? That's great!"

"The first practice is tomorrow after school," the man said. "See you then." He hung up, leaving Rob to wonder how in the world he'd heard about the Pirates' need for a coach so quickly.

Rob got out of bed to return the phone to its cradle. He thought about calling Benji to celebrate the good news but then saw how late it was.

I'll talk to him first thing tomorrow, he thought. Then he went to bed.

He woke up early the next morning. When he got downstairs, he grabbed the phone and opened the front door to get the morning paper for his mother to read. He'd punched in the first three numbers of Benji's phone number when the newspaper's top story caught his eye.

LOCAL HERO SAVES LIFE the headline

read in huge letters across the front page. Below the headline was his picture!

Rob hung up the phone and stared at the paper. That's how Mrs. Lasher found him.

"Goodness," she said when she saw what he was looking at. "I certainly didn't expect you to be the top story, did you?"

Rob shook his head and then began to read the article. Mrs. Lasher read over his shoulder.

"Well," she said when they were both through, "Ms. Carmichael certainly got the facts right. Reading this makes me prouder of you than ever! And that's really a great picture of you."

Rob nodded dumbly, still amazed by the prominence his story had gotten in the paper. "The funny thing is," he said at last, "I didn't even have to do the interview because Mr. Benoit had already signed on to be our coach!"

"Well, I think it's a marvelous story and well deserved, too. Here, let me have it. I want to send it to your father."

All through breakfast, Rob wondered who else had seen the story. He found out the minute he walked into school that morning.

"Hey, look, it's Rob!" a loud-mouthed girl cried. Rob recognized her as Ming's twin sister. "Will you sign my backpack?" She handed him a marker and then turned so he could scrawl his name on her bag.

That's how things went on all day. Kids he didn't even know slapped him on the back and congratulated him. Teachers complimented him, too. And at the end of the day, the principal got on the loudspeaker and asked that everyone take a moment to applaud their local hero, Rob Lasher. All the attention was too much for Rob.

Rob couldn't wait to get to soccer practice. There, at least, he hoped he'd be treated normally! He caught sight of Benji heading into the locker room to get ready for practice. Rob hadn't seen him or talked to him all day. Now he barreled toward him.

"Thanks a lot, Benji!" he said when he reached the other boy.

Benji stared at Rob in surprise. "What did I do?"

"The newspaper article!"

"But I didn't —" Benji started to say. Then his gaze shifted from Rob to someone behind him and he snapped his lips shut again.

At the same moment, Rob felt a hand drop on his shoulder.

"Are you the Lasher boy?" a gravelly voice rumbled behind him.

Rob turned to find a short, bald man behind him. The man was wearing a bright yellow T-shirt with the words STAN'S AUTO REPAIR emblazoned above a picture of a sad-faced car.

"I just read about you in the paper," the man continued. "I'm Coach Stan. Here, this is for you." He handed Rob a duplicate of the T-shirt he was wearing. He gave one to Benji, too, and then gestured to a box full of more shirts.

"Pass these out to everyone, will you, Lasher? Tell them to put them on and then do three laps around the field. I'll meet you out there." Coach Stan spun smartly and disappeared into the men's bathroom.

Rob stared at the shirt in his hands. Then he turned his back to Benji, took off the shirt he was wearing, and pulled the bright yellow one over his head. Then he turned back and looked at himself in dismay.

Benji covered his mouth with his hand to smother his grin.

"Oh yeah?" Rob jerked a shirt over Benji's head. "How do you like it!"

When Benji's head popped out the neck-hole, he was making a goofy face. Any rancor Rob felt for Benji vanished in that moment. They collapsed against each other, howling with laughter. When the other boys came to see what was so funny, Rob and Benji tossed shirts to each of them — and as they made their way to the field for the laps, everyone was whooping and shouting.

But their good humor vanished soon after. Coach Stan appeared just as they finished the last lap. "Okay, how about some jumping jacks?" he called from the sideline. "Let's say fifty?"

"Is he asking us or telling us?" Sam whispered.

"I guess he's telling us," Rob whispered back. "Come on."

After the jumping jacks, Coach Stan had

them do some push-ups and leg lifts. When they were through, the coach gestured to Rob.

"Lasher! Front and center!"

"Me, coach?"

The coach nodded, so Rob stepped forward.

"Okay, guys, here's the thing," the coach said, spreading his hands. "I know cars, not soccer. But you needed a coach, so here I am. That being said, I'm going to need someone who knows this game inside and out to steer me and this team right."

He jerked a thumb at Rob. "From what I read, this here's the guy to help me out. So unless there are any objections, I'm appointing him team captain. Okay?"

Kirk immediately started clapping. Others applauded, too, including Benji, who had a wide grin on his face. Rob grinned back.

But his smile faded when he saw Dmitri and Scott exchange looks. Neither was clapping and then Rob noticed that a few other boys were only applauding halfheartedly. Their message was loud and clear — the coach may have chosen Rob for their captain, but Rob wasn't their choice. Not by a long shot.

8

Now that that's settled," Coach Benoit said, "let's get started. How about you set up two lines of cones for a dribbling drill, captain?"

So Rob picked up the stack of orange cones and lined them up from the center line to the goal area. Meanwhile, the rest of the team divided into two groups for the drill. Rob lobbed three balls to each group and then trotted to the back of one line. Coach Stan stood at the side, leaned forward with his hands on his knees, and blew a loud shriek on his whistle. The first boy in each line took off, dribbling and slaloming between the cones.

Normally, the boys at the back of the lines would have chatted and joked around while waiting their turns. Today they were silent. A few looked at Rob, only to look away again quickly.

One after another, the boys finished the runs and returned to the ends of the lines. Then it was Rob's turn. He dribbled quickly to the first cone, and then nudged the ball sideways with his right foot, sending it to the left of the cone. He caught the ball on the instep of his left foot and with a sharp tap, redirected it past the cone. Then he picked it up with his right foot again and continued on to the next cone. When he'd made it through all seven, he gave the ball a vicious kick and sent it spinning into the open net.

He had just moved to retrieve the ball when *wham!* another ball slammed into his side.

"Oof!" The impact sent the air whooshing out of his lungs.

"Nice block." Scott hurried into the net, grabbed his ball, and ran out again without another word.

Rob picked up his own ball and returned to his line. As he did, he saw Scott glance over at him, nudge Arnold, and grin. Arnold looked at Rob, put his hands together, and gave him a mock-bow. Dmitri caught the move and started laughing.

Rob flushed from his toes to his scalp. Then he felt someone tap him. "Yo, dude," Raul said, pointing at the ball still in Rob's hands, "you gonna marry that ball or you want to give it up so I can take my turn?"

Embarrassed, Rob handed the ball to Raul, who placed it on the ground and took off through the cones.

Scott, Dmitri, and Arnold started laughing again. Rob stared at his feet.

The drill continued for several more minutes. Rob was beginning to wonder if the coach was planning to have them do the same thing for the entire practice. Then there was another whistle blast and Rob heard the coach call his name again.

"Okay, Lasher, break them into two teams for a full-field scrimmage," the big man said.

"A scrimmage, coach?" Rob asked, surprised. When Coach Brennan ran a practice, he usually worked on a few skills first. Then, if there was time, he had the team scrimmage so they could practice those skills in a game situation.

Coach Stan crossed his arms over his chest. "What, you got another idea?"

Rob remembered several kinds of drills Coach Brennan used to run. But he couldn't tell if Coach Stan really wanted to hear his suggestions or not. And he wasn't too sure he wanted to suggest them, not with the whole team listening. So instead he just stammered, "Um, no sir. A scrimmage sounds great."

It wasn't great. In fact, it was a disaster.

Rob had tried to make the teams even and to put players in the positions they were used to playing. Dmitri was in the center forward position. He faced Raul, whom Rob had put in the same position on the other team. On either side of Dmitri were Arnold and Scott. Behind him were two midfielders, Sam and Benji, and two fullbacks, Brendan and Ming. Raul had Leo to his left and Kirk to his right, Rob and Joey at midfield, and Bryan and Rudy at fullback.

Coach Benoit put the ball in the center circle and stepped back. Nothing happened. "Right, forgot to blow my whistle," the coach chuckled.

"Uh, no, coach," Rob called. "You should pick which side you want to start with the ball. Our old coach usually flipped a coin."

"Oh, okay!" The coach dug a coin from his

pocket. "Heads, Rob's team gets the ball, tails the other side." It came up heads.

"Now I can blow my whistle, right?" Coach Benoit blew a blast before anyone could answer.

Raul tapped the ball over to Leo. Leo started downfield at a fast clip, only to be stopped by Benji, who stripped the ball from him and sent it up to Dmitri. Dmitri flew across the center line, heading right toward Rob.

Rob danced on his toes, trying to anticipate if Dmitri would dodge around him with the ball or pass off to a teammate before he reached him.

Dmitri didn't do either. He continued straight for Rob. At the last moment, Rob had to jump out of the way or else be flattened! Only after Rob had moved did Dmitri send the ball to Scott — who, Rob saw, was standing right beside the net! Scott was obviously offside, but it was just as obvious that Coach Benoit didn't realize that.

Scott caught the ball on his foot and with a vicious kick laced it into the net.

"Well, well!" the coach cried, clapping madly. "Nice work, boys!"

Dmitri drew alongside Rob. "Say, captain," he drawled in a low voice. "You going let me get away with that? Or are you going to squeal to your new best friend, Mr. Auto Parts?"

After that, the scrimmage went straight downhill, and not just because the coach didn't know the rules of the game. It was a disaster because half the players had decided to side with Dmitri. Whenever someone loyal to Dmitri got the ball, he made sure to work a play with another one of Dmitri's followers, excluding those who seemed more inclined to side with Rob.

Of course, once the other players caught

on, they started excluding any player who sided with Dmitri! It got so bad that when one of Rob's players got the ball, his followers on the opposite team would stand back and let him make the play — even if it meant watching their own teammates struggle to stop them.

Thankfully, the practice ended sooner than usual.

"What was going on out there?" Benji asked incredulously as he and Rob headed back to the locker room.

"Isn't it obvious?" Rob spat. "Half of the team hates me!"

"Why would they hate you?"

Now Rob was incredulous. "Are you kidding? They hate me because the coach chose me to be captain instead of Dmitri. That stupid newspaper article is to blame! If he hadn't read it, he wouldn't have known me from any other player."

He gave Benji an angry look then. "Next time, Benji, check with me before you give my name to a reporter, okay?"

Benji stared at him, openmouthed. "I didn't give your name to anyone, Rob! Honest!"

The anger Rob felt left him like air leaving a balloon with a hole. "You didn't? How did that lady hear about what I did? And how come she knew we needed a coach?"

"I don't know, Rob," Benji said. "But it wasn't from me. I promise!"

Rob was completely mystified. He'd been sure Benji had been the one to contact the reporter. But he put aside his curiosity about the article very soon. There were more important things to worry about — chiefly, how to get the team back on track and how to turn Stan Benoit into a real coach!

9

Any hope Rob had that things would settle down on the team faded as the week went by. In fact, if anything, things got much worse. Part of the trouble was that Coach Stan continued to rely on Rob to help him. That just added fuel to Dmitri's fire, and to those of his followers. With the coach still not up to par with the game and half the players ignoring all Rob had to say, the season was beginning to look mighty grim.

Then came their first game. They were playing against the Sharks. Rob expected that by the time the game ended, the Sharks would have sunk their sharp teeth into the Pirates more than once.

The afternoon sun shone brightly on the field, making the chalk lines stand out crisp and white against the green grass.

"At least we don't have to wear those awful T-shirts today," Kirk called to Rob as Rob ran onto the field. "I like this one much better!"

Rob looked down at the black shirt with bold white lettering and nodded. *That's something I think the whole team would agree with,* he thought. *I hope it's not the only thing,* he added silently.

Rob took his position at right midfield and looked at the forward line. Scott was in front of him, at right, Dmitri was at center, and Raul was on his left. Last year, those three had been a nearly unstoppable offensive force. But this year, Raul had sided with Rob, making Dmitri and Scott angry. Rob wondered if they would include Raul in their attacks on goal or if they would leave him to work alone, as they had done during practices.

Then Rob glanced at his other midfielders, Joey and Benji. Joey was Dmitri's man all the way. Rob couldn't tell with Benji, however. Even though they were best friends, Benji hadn't thrown his hat in Rob's ring. He hadn't thrown it in Dmitri's either, however. In fact, now that Rob thought about it, Benji was probably the only player not to have chosen sides.

Behind the midfielders were fullbacks Ming — a Dmitri supporter — and Brendan, who gave Rob a thumbs-up when he saw him looking at him. Bryan was in the goal.

The Sharks won the toss and started off with a solid boot to right field. Rob and Joey double-teamed the right forward, but the Shark was too quick for them. He side-kicked the ball back to center before they had a chance to get it.

"Come on, captain, what's your problem?" Dmitri shouted as he chased the Shark center forward. "How about you try helping your teammate for once?"

Benji rushed over then and, before the Shark knew what was happening, stripped the ball from him and sent it to Raul in left field. Dmitri spun back and took off to join Raul in the attack.

Rob, Joey, and Benji stayed alert, ready to act if a Shark got the ball and tried to move the play to the other half of the field.

Raul made it deep into Shark territory before being threatened. He looked up, frantic to get rid of the ball. But Dmitri and Scott didn't seem interested in helping him. So Raul had no choice but to try to score. Unfortunately, he had a terrible angle on the goal. The ball floated through the air directly across the opening and bounced into the far corner, where a Shark fullback nabbed it.

One kick later and the ball streaked down the left field line with the Shark left forward running after it.

Joey and Benji ran forward to stop the drive. Benji got there first, but he muffed the play. Now Joey was a step behind the Shark forward and losing ground.

Ming was ready, however. He lunged in front of the Shark and slowed him down. Ming couldn't get his foot on the ball, though, for the Shark had passed to his center forward. That player deftly kicked to his right forward, who had rushed to a hole between Rob and Brendan.

Boom! The Shark delivered an instep kick that had Bryan sailing, hands outstretched, through the air in an attempt to stop it.

"Oof!" Bryan landed hard on his chest, having missed making the save by inches.

The Sharks whooped, delighted to have drawn first blood.

"Where were you, Lasher?" Dmitri growled. "Busy giving another interview somewhere, or doing something heroic again?"

"Lay off, Dmitri," Benji interjected. "That Shark came out of nowhere — this time, anyway. Rob, keep an eye on him so he can't fool you again!"

"Okay," Rob said.

Dmitri set up at the center circle again. Once more, he sent the ball toward Scott.

Big surprise, Rob thought as he trotted down the field.

Scott dribbled quickly and was met by two Sharks. He tried to maneuver around them but couldn't. Dmitri was covered, too, so Scott sent the ball back to Benji.

Benji moved fast toward the center of the field. He faked a pass to Joey but instead booted the ball to Raul. Raul, a surprised look on his face, almost didn't make the pickup. But after a bit of a foot fumble, he gained control and streaked down the open field with Rob close behind.

"Dmitri, give him a hand!" Benji cried.

Dmitri hesitated for a moment. Then he dodged around his defender and got open.

"Raul, find him!" Benji shouted.

Raul grimaced but kicked a solid pass to Dmitri. Dmitri trapped it and, with a twist of his body, blasted the ball into the outside corner of the net.

"Yes!" Benji yelled. "That's the way we do it!"

Normally, Raul and Dmitri would have exchanged high fives and bumped fists after such a success. But this year, they merely glanced at each other and then returned to their positions.

That's how it went for much of the game. Benji would call out suggestions for plays that required feuding teammates to work together. Sometimes the players listened. Sometimes they didn't. But Benji didn't give up. He just kept trying to get his teammates to play as a team.

In the end, however, nothing Benji or any of the other Pirates did helped. They lost to the Sharks by a dismal eight goals to one.

"Too bad, team, better luck next time," was all Coach Benoit said. Then he turned back to the man he'd been talking to and said, "So you think your car needs a new battery? Well, come on down to my shop and I'll set you up, no problem!"

"I sometimes wonder why that guy wanted to coach our team," Sam commented in a low voice.

Arnold snorted. "To drum up business for his shop, if you ask me. Because it sure isn't to win games!"

"Aw, come on, guys, don't be like that," Benji said. "I'm sure the guy's heart is in the right place — even if he doesn't know much about soccer!"

Rob shook his head. "Benji, you amaze me. We just got eaten alive by those Sharks, but you're still in a good mood. Why?"

"I guess it's because I know the Pirates have the potential to be better than we are right now," Benji shrugged. "I believe that we'll pull it together again, Rob. Simple as that."

And in that moment, Rob suddenly realized who the captain of the team should be. It wasn't him, that was for sure. And it wasn't Dmitri, either, although Dmitri was the best player.

No, the captain of the team should be someone who was willing to rise above all the bickering they'd been doing. Someone who wanted to see the team working as a unit again, like they had the year before.

Someone who had worked hard right from the start to keep the team together.

That someone, Rob knew, was Benji. He made up his mind, right then and there, to do what he could to make his friend's belief come true.

That night, when Rob got home from the game, he found the telephone directory and looked up two numbers. He took a deep breath and dialed the first number.

"Don't hang up, just listen to what I have to say," he said when the person he was trying to reach answered.

When he finished that conversation, he hung up and dialed the second number. That call lasted much longer and was much more exhausting but just as satisfying as the first had been.

There, he thought as he put the phone back in the cradle. *Now let's see what happens next!*

10

Rob could hardly wait for soccer practice the next afternoon. But when the time came for him to do what he wanted to do, he became very nervous.

What if this doesn't work? he thought.

Then he caught the eye of one of his teammates. The boy smiled at him and gave him the thumbs-up. It was just the encouragement he needed.

As usual, Coach Stan had Rob lead the team in three laps around the field and then had them do jumping jacks, push-ups, and leg lifts. When they were through, he called for Rob to set up a passing drill.

"Um, Coach Stan? Before we begin there's something I need to do," Rob said. He stood up in front of the rest of the team.

"Yes, Lasher, what is it?" the coach prodded.

"I need to resign as captain."

A ripple of surprise and confusion spread through the players. Coach Stan looked confused, too.

"What's this all about, Lasher?" he demanded. "You're not quitting the team, are you?"

"Oh, no sir!" Rob said hurriedly. "It's just that there's someone more qualified for the job."

"No kidding," Rob heard Scott mutter. He also heard Dmitri shush his friend.

Then Dmitri got to his feet. "I agree with Rob," the dark-haired boy said. "There is someone who'd make a much better captain than him."

Scott gave a cheer. "And we know who that is, don't we, D-man?"

Dmitri frowned. "Yeah, but it's not me, either, Scott."

"Wha —?"

Rob wished he had a camera to capture the look on Scott's face. "The guy we're talking about," he said, "is Benji."

Now it was Benji's turn to look surprised and confused. "Who, me? Why?"

"Because you're the only kid on this team who bothered to do anything to keep us together," Dmitri told him. "Signs, newspaper ads, calling the soccer league — you got the ball rolling that landed at Coach Stan's feet. He wouldn't be here if it wasn't for you, Benji. None of us would!"

"Not only that," Rob added, "but when we all started fighting and messing up as a team, you worked really hard to make us start working together again." Rob looked from face to face. "I may have helped save the coach's life and gotten my picture in the paper" — he fixed his gaze on his friend again — "but Benji, you're the real hero on this team! You're the one who's got my vote for captain."

"I second that!" Dmitri said.

"Third!" cried Kirk. And one by one, the other players added their voices. Benji was voted captain of the Pirates in a landslide.

Coach Stan scratched his head. "Okay, well, now that that's settled, how about we play some soccer?"

"Sure, coach," Benji said, "but now that I'm captain I'd like to make a couple of suggestions."

The coach nodded for him to continue.

"Right," Benji said. "First, we need to do more drills that help us perfect our basic skills. Then we need to come up with some really solid plays. I've been going on an awesome website that has some cool stuff I know we can do! If you want, I can print them out for you to see. And if you like them, we can work on them during practices until we've got them down cold."

"Okay," Coach Stan said. "Let's do it! Oh, and Benji, I'll take the address of that website. Maybe it'll help me make some sense of this game!"

"Hands in the middle, Pirates!" Benji cried, putting his arm out straight. The other players jumped to their feet and put their hands on top of his. Coach Stan put his in, too.

"Go, Pirates, fight!" Benji shouted.

"Just not with each other," Rob added with a smile.

The next week's practices were the best they'd had since Coach Brennan's heart attack. Benji showed them a few of the plays he'd found, and together they worked on them until they could do them in their sleep. When they suited up for their second game of the season, this time against the Black Hawks, they were all pumped and ready for action.

As Rob jogged onto the field, he glanced over to the stands. His mother had said she'd videotape the game so she could send it to his father. He spotted her high in the bleachers, camera in hand, and waved.

Then he saw someone else. His jaw dropped.

"Benji! Look! It's Coach Brennan!"

The boys swarmed around their old coach and peppered him with questions. At last, Coach Brennan laughed and shooed them onto the field. "You're going to miss the start of the game!" he said. His voice wasn't quite as booming as it had once been, but his grin was just as wide.

"Come on, guys, let's win it for Coach Brennan!" Benji roared. "And for Coach Stan, too!"

They hustled to their positions. Their side had won the toss so Dmitri readied the ball. As he waited for the referee's whistle, he caught Rob's eye and gave a slight nod. Then he did the same to Raul.

Rob's heart started pounding. Those nods were the signal for them to do one of their new plays! He crouched low and prepared for what was coming.

The whistle blasted. Raul charged toward Dmitri, looking for all the world as if he were to receive the kick-off pass.

Rob, meanwhile, edged sideways until he was close to Joey at the center of midfield.

"Here we go," Joey murmured.

Boom!

Dmitri kicked the ball hard — not sideways toward Raul, however, but behind him, toward Joey and Rob!

The Hawks defense was thrown off guard, just as the Pirates hoped they would be. While a few of them followed the ball, Raul cut back to the sideline. Joey, meanwhile, dribbled forward and dropped the ball, leaving it behind him for Rob to pick up.

Rob dragged the ball sideways with his left foot until he was closer to the right sideline.

"Hey! That kid's got it! Who's covering him?" a Hawk screamed.

At that same moment, Rob blasted a kick straight up to Raul. Raul caught it on the fly and tore up the field with the ball.

Dmitri, Joey, and Scott raced downfield as well. It was a risky move, including Joey in the charge, because it left a hole in the defense.

The risk paid off, however. Joey dodged

through all but one defender and planted himself near the front of the goal. Then he turned toward Raul, who at the same time was lofting the ball high in the air.

Rob held his breath. Was Raul's kick accurate?

It was! Joey, the best header they had on the team, leaped. The ball met his forehead and ricocheted toward the net.

The goalkeeper jumped, his arms outstretched.

Clang!

Rob and the rest of the Pirates groaned.

The ball had struck the crossbar.

Then suddenly — "YES!"

Dmitri was there fielding the rebound! The goalkeeper couldn't recover in time! The ball bounced off Dmitri's chest and, amazingly, dribbled into the goal just as the goalie made a desperate dive to try to keep it out.

"Whoo-hoo!" Benji cried. "It worked!" He pumped his fist and jabbed the air with a single finger.

Dmitri, Joey, and Raul hugged one another and then, still smiling, hurried back to their positions.

"We're going to win this one, big time," Benji predicted.

That prediction came true. By the end of the game, the Pirates had chalked up four goals. The Hawks had put in only one. Coach Stan was bubbling with the excitement, saying over and over how pleased he was to be part of such a terrific team.

"And to think, I only volunteered for this position to drum up business for my shop! Who knew being a coach could be so rewarding?"

After the game, Rob found Coach Brennan. "It sure was good of you to come," he said.

"I hope to make a few more," the coach said. "Oh, by the way, my wife wondered if you'd sign something for her?" He reached into a bag at his side and pulled out a clipping of Rob's newspaper article. "She wants to put it in her scrapbook. Do you mind?"

"Heck, no," Rob responded. He took the pen Coach Brennan offered and signed his name in a corner. "That okay?"

"Just right." The coach tucked the article away and then said, "So, what did you think of Ms. Enid Carmichael? She's something, isn't she?"

"You know her?"

The coach chuckled. "She's family. My wife's sister, actually. When Mrs. Brennan told her what you had done —"

"Hold on!" Rob interrupted, his eyes wide. "You mean the reporter heard about me through your wife? It all makes sense now!"

Then Rob started laughing and added, "I

guess I could have just called you to get her number instead of looking in the phone book."

"Her number? Why'd you need it?"

Rob scanned the crowd and then pointed. "I thought she might like to have a follow-up story to the one she wrote about me!"

The coach squinted. "Is that Enid? Who's that she talking to?"

Rob grinned. "She's interviewing the real hero of the Pirates — Benji!"

Coach Brennan gave a whistle. "I don't envy him. That woman can dig deeper than a treasure seeker after a golden statue!"

"You don't have to tell me that, coach," Rob said. "I've been there, remember?" He gazed at Benji and grinned again. "And if I have my way, I'll never be there again!"

The coach tapped his chest and smiled, too. "Yeah, there's one thing I'd rather not do again either." Then he gave Rob a gentle punch in the arm. "But if I ever do, I sure hope you or someone like you will be there to help. And in case I haven't said it before, Rob . . ."

Rob looked at the coach then.

". . . thank you for being a hero that day."

The two looked at each other for a long moment. Then Rob gave a half shrug.

"You're welcome, sir," he said simply.

THE #1 SPORTS SERIES FOR KIDS

MATT CHRISTOPHER®

Read them all!

- Baseball Turnaround
- The Basket Counts
- Body Check
- Catch That Pass!
- Catcher with a Glass Arm
- Comeback of the Home Run Kid
- Dirt Bike Racer
- Dirt Bike Runaway
- Football Double Threat
- Football Nightmare
- Goalkeeper in Charge
- The Great Quarterback Switch
- Halfback Attack*
- The Hockey Machine
- The Home Run Kid Races On
- Hook Shot Hero
- Hot Shot
- Ice Magic
- Johnny Long Legs
- Karate Kick
- The Kid Who Only Hit Homers

- Lacrosse Firestorm
- Long-Arm Quarterback
- Long Shot for Paul
- The Lucky Baseball Bat
- Miracle at the Plate
- Out at Second
- Power Pitcher**
- QB Blitz
- Return of the Home Run Kid
- Skateboard Renegade
- Skateboard Tough
- Slam Dunk
- Snowboard Champ
- Snowboard Maverick
- Soccer Duel
- Soccer Hero
- Soccer Scoop
- Spike It!
- Stealing Home
- The Submarine Pitch
- Tough to Tackle

* Previously published as Crackerjack Halfback
** Previously published as Baseball Pals

TWO PLAYERS, ONE DREAM...
to win the Little League Baseball® World Series

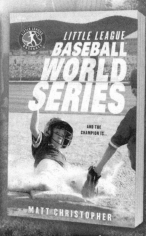

Read all about Carter's and Liam's journeys in the Little League series by MATT CHRISTOPHER.

LITTLE, BROWN AND COMPANY
BOOKS FOR YOUNG READERS

Discover more at lb-kids.com